THE WITCHES OF NORTH YORKSHIRE

"To disbelieve in witchcraft
is the greatest of heresies."
Malleus Maleficarum
(The Hammer of the Witches) 1486

Published by
East Coast Books
© The Caedmon Storytellers 2001

DEDICATED TO
MY MOTHER

COPY YE NOT THIS BOOKE IN ANY FORM
OR EVIL SHALL BEFALL THEE

A NOTE ON THE STORIES
THAT YOU MAY NOT BE OFFENDED

ALL of the stories in this book are drawn from TRADITIONAL SOURCES, and reflect the prejudices of the time of their origin. While we recognise that modern followers of WICCA may be young and beautiful, we feel that the haggard, hunched, WARTY, black-toothed, FOUL BREATHED, hairy legged, CROOKED NOSED, child scaring and BAD TEMPERED witches depicted in this book are too marvellous to be allowed to disappear for the sake of political or theological correctness. We hope you will show us tolerance, forgive, enjoy and even empathise with our entertaining book.

We also hope that the people of *Knaresborough* will forgive us for not including their most famous citizen, URSULA SOOTHELL or Mother Shipton. With so much written about her elsewhere, and with limited space in this book, we felt that other less illustrious witches deserved a chance.

THAT YOU MAY NOT BE OFFENDED
HEX DOUBLE HEX THRICE BACK RETURN
AND ABOUT AGAIN.

THE CAEDMON STORYTELLERS

CONTENTS

MAD MAGGIE OF WHITBY

MAD MAGGIE had a fearful reputation as a witch, but did not mind. Indeed she made her living by her AWFUL reputation. Her house was a dim cellar actually cut out of the rock in a little yard by the church steps. Children would flee when they saw her figure coming up the street, her black shawl over her head, her BEADY EYES blazing out.

The old people of the town were particularly afraid of Maggie, and for this reason: every year she kept the "vigil of St. Mark", sitting right through the night of April 24th in the porch of St Mary's where, so legend has it, the souls of those who are to die in the following year gather together. Everyone believed therefore, that Mad Maggie knew who was doomed to die in the following year. Maggie often paid a visit to her aged neighbours, and ELUDED to her supposed knowledge. They, fearful that *they* might be on the list, were always exceptionally generous to her, mistaking cause for effect, and believing that she might have an influence on "who was to go this year". If they made her a cup of tea, and she had a dissatisfied look on her face, they would offer her "a drop of something to liven it", adding a tot of rum or brandy. If she showed an interest in some small object or other, they would give it to her as a present.

The SAILORS and FISHERMEN of the town also felt that they should keep on the right side of Maggie, and to do so, they purchased pieces of string KNOTTED by her. These were no ordinary pieces of string, however, for when the knots were untied, (so she said), they would bring favourable winds to becalmed mariners. Maggie was always careful not to name a price for her pieces of string, leaving the decision to the customer, and looked displeased however much they paid. And this was for a very good reason too: a sailor, becalmed at sea would untie one of Maggie's knots. If a wind came, very well, he was pleased with his purchase. If however, no wind came, the sailor remembered Maggie's sour face and suspected that the wind had not come because he had not paid her enough, and made a note to be more generous the next time. So, strangely, the less effective her spells were, the more people paid her for them!

Perhaps her greatest trick, however, was to "bring" rain or sunshine to the local farmers. Maggie was an observant woman, and understood the SIGNS AND PORTENTS of the weather. If, for instance, after a spell of wet and windy weather the lobster pots stacked on the piers were covered with spider's webs one morning, then she knew from experience that good and settled weather was coming. She would immediately visit the local farms. There the farmer might complain to her that the wet weather was stopping him from cutting hay, and Maggie would seize the opportunity of offering to "bring" him a few days of sun for a certain fee.

By these and other deceptions, Maggie had the whole town in her thrall. Even the people who disbelieved in her power found it convenient to hide their scepticism as it would have been seen as implying that their neighbours were naive and foolish for buying charms etc from the old woman. Indeed the unbelievers often took the greatest care in protecting themselves against her, putting "witch-stones" (pebbles from the beach with natural holes through them), in their windows, to prevent her from crossing the threshold of their property. This was not because they believed in the power of witch-stones, but because Maggie herself was forced to avoid all such protected dwellings or have her credibility as a witch undermined.

Maggie was aware that she was not popular, those who did not believe in her powers thought she was a heartless swindler, and the believers resented her power over them. A few people even muttered darkly that the town would be a much better place if she was dead, but she did not fear that anyone would take it into their heads to hasten her death, for she took care to let everyone know of her prophesy that on the day she died, a great storm would lash the North Sea, and many a sailor or fishermen would never again their homes again.

It was a bright spring morning on the day that Maggie died, and COBWEBS festooned the lobster pots upon the pier. By mid day, great banks of heavy cloud had built up on the horizon, the wind had disappeared, and the sea had become flat and motionless. An ominous calm settled over the town. Even the seagulls were silent, They stared intently out to sea then turned and flapped away inland. That evening, a terrible storm came - the worst in living memory. Tiles were ripped from roofs and flung many hundreds of feet through the air, while the sea crack't against the cliffs so hard that the noise, like the cannons of a great army, could be heard many miles inland.

The following morning, in the midst of seaweed and wreckage, strange sea creatures, never before seen, were found dumped ashore. And many a Whitby fisherman or sailor, unlucky enough to be at sea on the day that Maggie died, perished in the storm, and never saw their homes again.

They made a trade of their reputation. They were the wise women of their day. They professed some knowledge of medicine, and could recover stolen property. People gave them money for their services. Their very threats brought silver into their coffers. It was in their interest to gain (an) ill name. Depositions from the castle of York p30

NANNY HOWE OF KILDALE

ONCE UPON A TIME lived an old witch by the name of
NANNY HOWE. She had a fat ginger cat called Moggy and a
bessom, or broom-stick, which she used to get around at night.
She did no-one much harm, except to change the occasional
child into a toad or snail if they annoyed her.

Her bessom was not only used for moving her about, it
also did most of her household chores. She would shout:
"BESSOM", and it would instantly fly to her hand. She would
whisper, "WATER", and the broom would go to the well and
return with a bucket of water, or "BESSOM, FLOOR.", and it
would sweep the floor. This useful implement left Nanny
Howe free to do what she liked the best: to grow herbs and
vegetables in her garden.

Now you might think that everyone would be happy
to leave a harmless witch like Nanny Howe alone, but her
harmless behaviour was not pleasing to one person, and that
person was THE DEVIL. The Devil, having given powers to
Nanny, expected some return for his generosity. He expected
to see sheep give birth to three-headed lambs, neighbour
turned against neighbour. In short he expected Nanny to creep
around as he did, spreading mischief.

The Devil decided to visit Nanny Howe and let her
know how he felt. He chose a dark and stormy night, as you
would expect, and knocked on her door just as the church
clock struck twelve. Nanny Howe was reading a seed

catalogue at the time, and was surprised that anyone should call so late, for she rarely had company. Well Nanny opened the door carefully, and let the Devil in, and he took a seat.

"Bessom" shouted Nanny Howe, "tea", and the bessom disappeared into the little kitchen and returned a few minutes later with a pot of tea. The Devil was not very pleased with the tea, for he felt that a witch should at least be addicted to strong drinks like RUM or WHISKEY. Nanny Howe could see he was not pleased, but mistaking the cause shouted: "Bessom, digestive biscuits!"

At this the Devil could restrain himself no more. "WELL", says the Devil, "what have you done with all my gifts? I came past here this week, and found the people happy, healthy crops in the fields, no plagues. I admit you have changed a few naughty boys into frogs and such like, but I find that the people of KILDALE are rather pleased to be rid of them: they were causing more trouble than you!

"And here I find you, drinking tea, growing vegetables, your house spick and span rather than a rat infested cobwebby hovel...."

At that moment Nanny Howe glanced down, and noticed that the Devil had brought mud in on the floor, she could see the marks of his cloven feet from one end of the room to the other.

"MY FLOOR!" she cried, "BESSOM!" Immediately the bessom flew to its mistress, and the Devil expected she would soon set it to work to clean the floor. Instead she brought it down on his head with such a crack that he fell down flat.

Now the Devil remembered why he had chosen Nanny Howe in the first place, for she had a terrible temper once roused. She went to hit him again, but he succeeded in getting hold of one end of the bessom, but this was a mistake, for Nanny let go the broom, and began to scratch his face so viciously that the Devil would have been blinded had he not dived out of the window, where he landed headfirst in Nanny's best manure heap. Nanny too dived out of the window, landed heavily on him and managed to kick his bottom twenty three times before he could get out of the manure.

The Devil realised he was in big trouble and decided to escape. He leapt over the church tower and went a HUNDRED MILES before he dared to look back. And there behind him, he saw Nanny Howe. For as soon as the Devil had taken to the air, she had called "Bessom", and climbed aboard. The Devil flew three times round the moon to escape from Nanny Howe, but with each loop he found she was nearer to him, and now he could see her face, snarling, vicious. His death must surely have followed had it not been for an imp, who saw his master was in trouble, and craftily jumped onto the back of the broom and slowed it down just enough for the Devil to make his escape.

Nanny Howe eventually gave up the chase, and went home instead to plant some carrots, and there she lives quietly with her BESSOM and her CAT to this day.

ANNE PIERSON *OF* GOATHLAND

PERHAPS the most ACTIVE witches in North Yorkshire were those of Goathland. Some families passed their witchcraft skills down from generation to generation. Anne Pierson came from one such family; her mother and grandmother were both supposed to be witches. She lived in a decrepit cottage on the edge of the village and had the reputation of having "THE EVIL EYE", an ability to harm people with a single glance. No one dared go near her hovel. Children would run away screaming even at the mention of her name, while their parents would cross the road to avoid the old witch. As a result, Anne, was a bitter and lonely old woman.

It was sometime during the nineteenth century that Goathland's squire discovered that his daughter had fallen in love with a local farm worker. He had plans to marry her to one of his wealthy neighbours and, knowing her to be a headstrong girl, feared she would elope with the boy if he made any objection to her romance.

The squire tried several way of breaking his daughter's affection for the poor farmworker; he organized a grand ball in his house, inviting all the rich and eligible young gentlemen from miles around, hoping she would fall for one of them; he even tried to have the lad pressed into the navy - but none of these ruses worked.

The squire was an educated man, and along with the other "important" people in the village, the doctor, the priest, the schoolmaster etc, had always scoffed at the notion that the mad old woman who lived in the old falling down ruin at the edge of the village was a witch. So it is an indication of how desperate he was that he made his way to her cottage one evening, after dark. Checking behind him to make sure that no-one had seen him coming, the squire knocked nervously at Anne Pierson's door. After a minute the old woman opened it an inch or so, and peered suspiciously at him. He told her he had come on "business", and with one boney finger, she summoned him inside.

The squire looked around the single, DINGY room which was her home. Feeble firelight flickered over her few sticks of rotten furniture. In a corner a few dirty blankets lay by a heap of straw which served as the witch's bed.

At this point the squire would have done well to consider why it was that the old woman lived in such miserable circumstances when the ignorant villagers credited her with so many powers. But his thoughts were interrupted when the old crone demanded to know what his "business" was. As the squire told her that he wanted something to stop his daughter from eloping, the old crone became excited, walking up and down the room, rubbing her hands GLEEFULLY, muttering under her breath.

In one corner of the room was a little wooden chest, and from it the old woman took a little bottle filled with a pale yellow liquid. She gave this to the squire, and told him to add the contents to his daughter's food.

The squire thrust a few guineas into the crone's hands, and made his way home by quiet paths so that no-one would know where he had been.

At supper that night the squire succeeded in adding the yellow liquid to his daughter's food. The following morning he was horrified to discover that his daughter was unlikely to elope, not because she had fallen out of love as he expected, but because she had become paralysed from the neck downwards!

Two doctors were called but neither could find a reason for her problem and both left, shaking their heads, BAFFLED. But the squire knew the cause, and was too ashamed to tell the doctors of his visit to the witch.

After pacing the house impatiently all through the day, the squire set off as darkness fell to see the witch again. He hammered on her door, but she would not open it to him, so he had to beg her to take off the spell through a little chink. The witch refused, dancing up and down behind the door, laughing. He offered her money, threatened to beat her, but to no avail. Finally in despair the squire turned to go home, a broken man.

Soon the girl's mysterious illness was the talk of the village, and the farm worker, hearing of it, and being from an old Goathland family, immediately suspected that the cause was witchcraft. And he knew what to do. He visited a local Wiseman, skilled in countering the spells of witches, and told him about the girl's symptoms. The WISEMAN gave him some tea. and afterwards told him to look at the leaves at the bottom of the cup and asked him if he could see a face there.

When the farm worker said that he thought he could

see a rough likeness of Anne Pierson, the Wiseman nodded his head in satisfaction.

The cure for the girl's troubles, according to Wiseman, was to mix some of the witch's blood with holy water, and to rub the girl's feet with it. The farm worker went home and considered what he should do. The problem was the blood. He couldn't ask Anne Pierson for some of her blood in order to break her spell, for she would be unlikely to cooperate, and besides, counter spells only worked if done secretly. Also if he attacked her with a knife and cut her, he would probably be sent to gaol.

Then he remembered that witches were known to turn themselves into HARES occasionally to go about causing mischief.

So he armed himself with a shotgun and some holy water that very night, and slipped into a field by Anne's cottage, where he waited in the shadows patiently. At midnight the biggest grey hare that he had ever seen appeared under Anne's hedge. Waiting for a few seconds to make sure he could not miss, the farm worker fired his gun, hitting the creature heavily in its back legs. The wounded animal, screeching in pain, dragged itself back under the hedge, leaving a GORY TRAIL OF BLOOD smeared over the grass. The farmworker jumped up and gathered some of this blood on a handkerchief, then ran to his sweetheart's house. He climbed in through her bedroom window with the aid of a ladder which he had hidden earlier. After waking the girl to tell her what he was doing, he poured some holy water onto the handkerchief and rubbed her feet. Immediately, her paralysis disappeared, and she was restored to full health. And now the squire's worst fear came to pass: for the ladder was then used by the couple to elope!

As for Anne Pierson, she was not seen for some days after this incident, and when eventually she did appear, she was seen to be HOBBLING with the aid of two walking sticks, bloody bandages wrapped around her HAIRY LEGS.

MARY BATEMAN
THE YORKSHIRE WITCH

THE witches of Scarborough and Rydale were numerous, but on the whole not quite so colourful as those to the north. With the exception of SABINA MOSS, (who had a boxing match with the devil and, being knocked senseless, fell into a slurry pit), most were strictly professional witches: in 1634, four women from West Ayton were tried for "taking it upon themselves to tell one, Barbara Temple, by witchcraft, charms or sorceries, where stolen clothes were to be found." MARY NARES of Pickering, PEGGY DUELL and NAN SCAIFE both from Hutton-le-Hole were all professional fortune tellers, though at least Nan Scaife made a bit of an effort: her "magic cubes" or dice were constructed from the ground skulls of hanged men, bullocks blood and crabs' eyes.

In Scarborough, Wisemen and Women acted almost like family doctors, checking symptoms, writing out prescriptions, (a sign of the Zodiac, a verse from Solomon's proverbs and a few dried beech leaves was the accepted cure for the evil eye).

So it is almost with relief that we turn to MARY BATEMAN. Mary was born just outside Thirsk, and from her earliest youth showed signs of future promise. From the moment she could walk, Mary began to steal. She became so notorious, that while still in her teens she had to move to Leeds to get a job, for no one closer would even consider employing her.

In Leeds Mary set up as a dressmaker and "soothsayer", and soon attracted a clientele of credulous people, whom she robbed and destroyed, heartlessly. On one occasion she convinced a woman with a large young family that her husband should enlist in the army. Soon afterwards, he was killed in the Napoleonic wars, and she was left penniless, committing suicide after her children died for want of medicines.

But it was her treatment of William and Rebecca Perigo which led to her lasting fame. Rebecca Perigo had an irrational fear of "the evil eye", and sought Mary's help. Bateman realising there was money to be had, soon made the couple bankrupt. She made them sell their furniture to obtain charms from "Mrs Blythe", a powerful but imaginary Wisewoman from Scarborough. She had them give her their life savings in gold sovereigns, which she wrapped in paper and sewed into Mrs Perigo's clothes. A simple conjuring trick allowed Mary to swap the coins for lead disks.

Once the Perigos were penniless, Mary had no more use for them, but since they kept coming to beg for her help and bothering her, she decided to get rid of them completely. In April 1807, she showed them a letter which "Mrs Blythe" had sent, along with seven packets of powder, and a jar of honey. Mrs Blythe's instructions were for the couple to lock themselves in their house for a week, and to take the powders she had provided, one each day. If they happened to feel sick, this was a sign that their "enemy" had found out what they were doing, and they should each eat half the honey she had thoughtfully provided to counter the attack.

The Perigos did as they were instructed, and for six

days encountered no problems. On the seventh day however, the powder which they ate contained a highly poisonous substance, Mercuric Chloride. Both were exceedingly ill, and opened the jar of honey. This contained another deadly poison, Arsenic. Mr. Perigo could not bear to eat more than a drop of the honey, but his wife, terrified of the supernatural forces which she felt were bearing down upon her, swallowed the lot, and died six days later, in dreadful agony.

Mr Perigo never suspected foul play even though his lips had turned black from eating the honey until, a few months later, he decided to get rid of his wife's clothes. He cut out the gold sovereigns which Mary had sewed into the hems, and was amazed to find lead disks. Suspicions raised, he contacted the magistrates then, with constables concealed, arranged to meet Mary once more. She was arrested, and in her bag was found a bottle of poison which she had intended to use on Mr. Perigo to silence him forever.

Mary was tried for murder, found guilty, and condemned to die. Even while waiting for her appointment with the gallows, she continued her cruel criminal career, selling forged pardons to other condemned criminals.

Bateman was hanged at York on the 20th March 1809, and so infamous was she, that the hangman had her body pickled, and took it on tour round the North of England, thousands of people turning up, and paying, to see the corpse. Finally, when her body began to disintegrate, her skin was peeled off and cured, strips of it being sold as charms against evil.

THE WITCH HUNTERS

THE night is cold. The full moon shines brightly on the village and glints in the water. A small procession of people can be seen, making their way down to the harbour side. Their moon shadows, moving in front of them, are strangely shortened. Their faces are serious, determined, and in their hands they carry flaming torches, sharp needles or pins. At the head of them, a man carries the heart of a freshly slaughtered cow, still steaming and dripping blood: the people of Staithes are out, searching for a witch.....

STAITHES folk are noted for their strange customs. Every year on a certain night the unmarried people parade round the village in their bedclothes, looking for a suitable husband or wife, while the vicar waits in his church ready to carry out the ceremony immediately.

They pour brandy and Christmas cake down the throat of the first FISH they catch in the new year then let it free, sure that it will tell its FRIENDS how well the men of Staithes treat the fish they catch, so that they all get caught on purpose.

And when anyone suffers from WITCHCRAFT, the townsfolk gather as we have seen, with flaming torches, sharp needles and a fresh cow's heart, all out to catch the witch.

Down at the dockside the grim procession halts. The torches are piled together to form a bonfire. Each of the victims of witchcraft takes a pin and sticks it into the cow's steaming heart, murmuring of the offence they have suffered. At last the heart is dropped into the flames. Blood boils from the vessels, hissing and popping. Thenn the heart takes fire, and a rich smell fills the air. Now is the moment. Now the witch must reveal herself.

The group looks about them, peering up little alleyways, and round corners. Then in the distance a figure emerges, pale and ghostly in the moonlight. Closer it glides, eyes open but seeing nothing. The figure, moving slowly, enters the group, and stops by the fire.

People begin to mutter. Here is the witch, no doubt of it, drawn by the powerful magic of the pierced heart. They all know her; she is from their little town, but not one of them had suspected she was the witch who had put so many terrible spells upon them.

"Spoilt my fishing," said one.

"Gave me terrible spots," says another.

"Ha," says a third, "that's nothing. She made my wife and bairns run away with the milkman!"

They all gaze at the motionless figure.

"Good job we caught her when we did. Who knows what else she would have done?"

"She'll cast no more spells after tonight, that's for sure."

Now the leader of the hunt approaches the woman, and takes her arm. GENTLY, he turns her around and, after pressing a penny into her hand, points her back from whence she came. Slowly, in a trance, she returns home, to wake the following morning surprised at finding her feet dirtied by walking, and a penny in her hand.

In Staithes, no blame is attached to a witch. Here it is believed that witches are created by some unknown and evil force to cast spells, unaware of what they do. The ceremony of the cow's heart not only identifies the accidental witch, but frees them from the evil spirit which possesses them.

And now her victims, having warmed their hands by the fire for a while, disperse to their homes, satisfied with a good night's work.

OLD KATTY
OF RUSWARP

OLD Katty lived in a wonderful time for witches, for the brutal laws against witchcraft had just been repealed, but the belief in witchcraft amongst country folk was still strong. Katty made the most of her evil reputation, terrifying the local population. None dared look her in the face, for they believed she had "The Evil Eye", and could cast spells on them with a wicked glance. If anyone had to talk to her, they did so in a very respectful manner, cap in hand, eyes looking down to the ground. As a result, Old Katty, old and smelly hag as she was, began to feel that she was rather better than her neighbours, and began to look down on them.

Now one day, much to every one's surprise, a ragged old PEDLAR, known as ABE ROGERS, came to Ruswarp, walked straight into Old Katty's cottage, sat in her best chair, put his feet on the table, dropped his pack on the floor and said:

"PUT THE KETTLE ON, YOU OLD WITCH!"

Today we do not see many pedlars, but at that time they were common enough. They bought a few packets of pins or other cheap articles in a town, then sold them round the country side, often telling a sad tale of misfortune to the country folk, so that in pity they would buy the goods whether they needed them or not. Pedlars often slept in hedges, and were very poor, all their worldly possessions carried on a pack over their shoulder.

The neighbours, forgetting for a while their fear of Old Katty, gathered near the door, all peering in. They saw the old woman meekly pick up the kettle, fill it, and put it over the fire, glancing nervously now and then at the pack. Everyone expected that once it boiled she would pour it over the pedlar's head, but were amazed when she mashed the tea and gave him a cup in her best china!

Murmering, amazed, they went home, wondering how Abe Rogers dared to treat Old Katty in this way. And from their wondering and muttering, a *LEGEND* grew.

THE LEGEND OLD KATTY PEDLAR

Once upon a time there lived in **RUSWARP** a powerful witch called "Old Katty". Old Katty had many powerful spells and had as her familiars, **TWENTY THREE** huge demons to carry out her will. One day while walking up on the hills by a tiny bridge over a little stream over which only one person could cross at a time, she came upon a pedlar known as Abe Rogers. Old Katty thought that she, a powerful witch with twenty three huge demons to carry out her will was very much better than a mere pedlar, and although he was already on the bridge, she told him to stand aside and let her across. Abe ignored her command and carried on. The old witch jumped up onto the bridge to block his way, but the pedlar yanked her up by her collar and dumped her into the stream. Old Katty was furious. She waded to the bank, and pulled out a knife ready to cut him to pieces. He however simply laughed, knocked the knife out of her hand, and tripped her into a muddy patch. Old Katty, now in a crimson rage, decided to use her supernatural powers to gain revenge. She muttered a few secret words, and immediately twenty three great Ugly Demons appeared in a circle round Abe Rogers. Katty shouted **"DON'T LET HIM GET AWAY!"**, and the awful creatures began to advance on Abe, baring great yellow teeth, red eyes gleaming. Old Katty rubbed her hands with glee, looking forward to seeing the upstart pedlar ripped limb from limb.

The pedlar dropped his pack, but not in fear. He pulled out a little wallet, and from this wallet plucked a tiny pinch of dust, which he threw straight up into the air. Suddenly a great whirlwind appeared, spinning the dust into the demon's faces who fell to the ground in agony, clutching at their eyes. Abe snatched up Old Katty's knife, cut off the left ears of the creatures, and popped them into his pack. He knew that by having part of their flesh and blood they could have no power over him. He picked up his pack, smiled mockingly at Old Katty, and went on his way.

After this, whenever he passed Ruswarp, Abe made a point of visiting Old Katty and making himself at home, putting his feet up on the table and shouting "PUT THE KETTLE ON YOU OLD WITCH!"

And he always got his tea too, for Old Katty, although she was hardly pleased to be addressed in this way, was too terrified of what else might be LURKING in the bottom of his pack to mutter or protest.

ELSIE BARBER

A CUNNING AND DETERMINED WITCH

IT WAS A COLD WINTER'S NIGHT in 1805 in the village of Danby. Candle light flickered in the corner of the bar of the Spit and Gristle, glinting on the pewter tankards of three men. Two of them had great gnarled features, the result of many years exposed to the rough winds and weather, for they were farmers, and it is a hard life farming on the NORTH YORK MOORS. The other man's features were softer, he was a foreigner, who had moved to the village a few years before.

"I see that poor old ELSIE BARBER has gone to her maker," he said.

"Gone SOMEWHERE ELSE, more like," said one of the gnarled farmers, "for she was a rum un."

"Ay, she was", said the other, "tell us about your sheep, George, for I think our friend William here, being a foreigner, don't know about our Elsie."

"Well," says George, "I will. It must be eight years now since I taught that witch such a lesson as she shan't forget. Now I'd always thought she was a WITCH, People said she could turn herself into a HARE and go about causing mischief, and although I never spoke to any one who actually saw her make the change, I never had any reason to doubt it was true, because if so many people believe a thing, why it must be true, mustn't it?"

John, the other farmer, nodded his head and said "Ay and they say she suckled a pair of imps with three eyes, and that's true as well, for everyone says it is."

"Now," continued George, "she came up to our farm one cold morning, a begging for bread. Her, who could summon up the devil any time she wanted to lay her out a feast as would make your eyes boggle! My wife turned her away, of course, for it would not do to go feeding a witch, even if she claimed to be a poor old widow with no-one to support her in her old age. Well Elsie limps off down the lane with her crooked leg, and immediately the wife begins to feel not right, guilty like, for sending her off WITHOUT A SCRAP OF FOOD, and clad only in a few thin rags".

"Yes," breaks in John, "it was a bad winter that year, the snow stood on the ground right through the winter, and you'd often see old Elsie's foot prints in it - for she had no shoes, and went round the farms barefoot, begging for food."

"Ay" says George, "no shoes - her that could summon the devil any time she wanted to give her a hundred pairs of shoes, gold slippers too, I should think if she wanted.

"Well as I said, the wife was FEELING A BIT GUILTY, and would have gone down the lane to fetch her back for sure, but I says, that Elsie is putting a spell on you, making you feel that way- and I was right, for Elsie was so mad that I stopped the wife, that three months later, she cursed one of my sheep, and it fell ill."

"How do you know that it was Elsie made it ill?" asked the foreigner, surprised.

"Ha," laughed George, "how do I know? Why, it was a healthy animal, and why should it fall ill unless it had a curse put on it? And who was going to put a curse on it if it wasn't

"Anyway, I wasn't having it, so I went out and found Elsie, sleeping in a ditch as usual. Her, sleeping in a ditch, who could summon up the devil any time she wanted and make her a house, a gold palace, even I wouldn't be surprised. "Well I told her straight, if she didn't take the curse off my sheep, I'd drag her into the market place and whip her in front of the whole village.

"But come market day the sheep is still ill! So I finds old Elsie and drags her to village, and I asks her straight, will she take the curse off my sheep?"

"Aye, he did, I remember it well." Says John.

"Then you'll also remember what she said too, eh, John? Why she says she doesn't know anything about my sheep, the cheek! She denies it to my face. So I whipped her there in the market place, fifty good lashes with my bull whip, but would you believe it, though that whip is so heavy I could make a team of oxen jump through a hoop with just one taste of it, it doesn't make any impression on Elsie, even though she screams blue murder, and bleeds a bucket of blood on the market place, for when I get home, the sheep's still ill.

"Why I was so mad, I came back to the market, and finds old Elsie, lying on the ground groaning, pretending that she can't walk. Well, I picks her up and brings her in here, and gets the landlord to lock her in the cellar, telling her that if my sheep is not better by next market day, that I'll give her a better whipping than the last.

"Isn't that true, landlord?" he shouted to the bar.

"Ay, it is," replies the Landlord, and coming over to

them says in a low voice, "I NEVER TOLD ANYONE THIS BEFORE, but old Elsie did me some mischief while she was locked in the cellar: A few nights later a traveling man came here, and left without paying his bill!"

"Oh she was a wicked one, that Elsie," says John.

"But," says the foreigner, "maybe the traveller would have robbed you anyway."

The landlord looked at him, puzzled for a second.

"Well, maybe, for I'd been robbed before, but maybe them robberies also came about from witchcraft eh? For", he said, dropping his voice further "there's a lot of witches about, you know."

George and John began to look around the room nervously now, peering into corners to see if there were any suspicious characters lurking there.

"Now," says George, "the next market day comes around, and my sheep is no better, so out I drags Elsie, her screaming MERCY, MERCY, all the while, and gives her a whipping which would kill an ox. There was two hundred people there to watch, for it had got about what I was going to do, and with each lash a great cheer goes up, and I whipped her until my poor arm ached. In the end, we had to pour buckets of cold water on her to keep her awake for she was almost dead.

"Then I says will she take the curse off my sheep? Would you believe it, she was so stubborn, that when I get home my sheep is still poorly, worse even. Still, I think, she's locked in the cellar, she can't go anywhere, we'll see who gets tired of this business the first."

Now the foreigner interrupted him "But surely it is illegal to lock someone up in a cellar?"

"Oh maybe, but who was she to complain to? Why the Justice of the Peace is a farmer himself, and doesn't look kindly on people laying spells on livestock. Why he would have had her hanged if she had complained to him!

"So, I kept her locked in that cellar for over a month, whipping her every week, (and one extra time, when the fair was in town, and everyone wanted to see Elsie whipped), and still my sheep didn't improve.

"Any way, on the Sunday, after I'd lashed her a good six or seven times, I looks out of the window and see that Elsie has come to her senses, for the sheep is up on it's feet and feeding as well as it ever did, so I came down to the village and let her go. And do you know, she said from first to last that she had nothing to do with my sheep!"

The foreigner looked perplexed. "Maybe that's the truth, maybe the sheep just got better by itself", he said.

George looked thoughtful at this, and began to rub his chin, then turned to the foreigner, "You know, I never would have thought of that, maybe I let her go without her ever lifting the curse! Well then, if so, she got off very lightly, for I'd have happily whipped that witch 'til she was nothing but a bag of bones."

"No, what I mean is maybe Elsie didn't have anything to do with making your sheep ill, or making it better again. Maybe she was just a poor old lady."

"What, her poor that could summon up the devil any time she wanted to give her gold and silver - diamond necklaces too I wouldn't be surprised, and that changed into a hare to do mischief, and sent strangers to rob the ale house!"

"But she didn't have any gold, as far as I could see" replied the foreigner.

"Of course not, she was a poor old widow woman, with no-one to support her, she had to go round the farms begging for bread didn't she? If she'd had a pile of gold, why we'd all have known she was a witch. CUNNING, you see."

"Ay," says John, nodding, "CUNNING AND DETERMINED. Had to be locked in a cold cellar and whipped for a month before she'd take off the curse from George's sheep."

The foreigner looked at the two farmers and shook his head. "But why did she live in a ditch if she could have a house?"

"Cunning again, you see," said John.

The foreigner got up to go, still shaking his head in disbelief, he finished his beer, and bid them good night.

After he was gone, the two farmers began to nod to each other, agreeing that foreigners were a funny lot.

"Didn't believe it about old Elsie, did he, George? Even though it's as plain as the nose on your face she was a witch."

"Ah, it's through living in a City, John, that's it: terrible big wicked place, that Grosmont!"

Monday Nov. 27 1797
George Langstaff soundly whipped Elsie Barber for causing an evil amang hys sheep, four died before he whipped her.

                    Entry from an old diary

OLD NAN'S REVENGE

OLD NAN was a homeless outcast who wandered over the North Yorkshire Moors, begging for her bread, or a place to sleep. Some people were kind, and fed her or pressed a penny or two into her hands, but the majority shunned her, said she was a DIRTY OLD WITCH, though no one had ever heard of her casting spells or cursing anyone.

There was once a TINKER, a mender and seller of pots and pans, who was making his way along a quiet road, The sun was just rising, for he hoped to be in Stokesley early to offer his services at the market. Pots and pans clanked merrily in his open cart as his old horse plodded along. Suddenly his horse halted, and Old Nan stepped out from a little byeway at the side of the road.

TIM SMITH, the tinker, had always suspected that Old Nan was a witch, and this confirmed his belief, for witches have the power to stop horses in their tracks. He smiled however, for he had a "witchwood" whip, and had only to wave it over the animal's head to break the old crone's power. He waved the whip, but nothing happened. Old Nan took the horse's bridle, and began to lead it down the little byway. He brought the whip down on her arm, but it passed harmlessly through her body!

Tim shook with fear, for he realised he was looking at a ghost, or worse; for along the track stood a little hill which had the reputation of being full of CRUEL FAIRIES, who sometimes dragged humans down into the hill, never to be seen again.

Nan stopped the horse at a little cave, and pointed. "It's for her," she whispered. "It's my treasure, I saved it for her."

Tim looked into the cave and saw hanging there five bags overflowing with GOLD COINS.

"You can have five coins for yourself," she said, "the best from each bag, but the rest you must take to my daughter. For, you see, they took her away from me when she was just a baby, on account of me being a little mad, and a beggar. It's all

I could ever do for my baby. You must help."

Tim looked fearfully at the cave - was it a trick? Would the entrance close up behind him when he entered, and the fairies grab him?

Eventually his GREED got the better of him. He ran in and grabbed the bags, and on each of the bags, clearly sewn in, was the name and address of Nan's daughter. Dashing out of the cave again, he looked around, but there was no sign of Nan.

TEN YEARS passed, and Tim was a tinker no more. He had put his five gold coins to good use, along with the rest of them, for he never delivered the bags to old Nan's daughter. He had become a rich merchant, and instead of driving a cart, he rode a thorough-bred horse.

One evening, Tim was riding out to take the air on the hills above Stokesley. He had gone out as far as he ever went: for he never passed the place where he had met Nan's ghost. He was just turning for home when, glancing over his shoulder, he saw the figure of OLD NANNY sitting on his horse's rump. In terror he began to thrash his whip at her over his shoulder, but the lashes passed through the spectre and into the flank of his lively thorough-bred. The horse immediately began to gallop wildly along the road in the direction which Tim never dared to go. Desperately, he tried to slow the horse, but with no success. It plunged on, maddened by his pulling of the reins.

Somewhere along the winding moorland road, Tim fell. Tangled in his stirrups, he was dragged along to his death.

The horse and its mangled rider were found the following day where a little byroad turns off from the main highway. The coroner's report into the "ACCIDENT" noted that the horse was grazing peacefully, but that Tim's battered corpse had an awful look about its face.

A look not of pain, but of DREADFUL TERROR.

BETTY STRUTHERS
OF CASTLETON

IT WAS TWILIGHT, and the condemned man sat in his cell, weeping. The sound of revelers who had come into town to watch the next day's hangings could be heard in the courtyard, along with the plaintive cries of women, soon to be widows, calling their husbands' names, hoping to catch one last glimpse of their beloved's face. It was not at these sad sounds that the prisoner, BENJAMIN CLARKE wept, however, but at the voice of BETTY STRUTHERS outside the door of his cell, haggling with the hangman, over the price of a dead man's hand.

In Thirsk there stands an ale house which was once the haunt of highwaymen and other wicked characters. The thieves would gather on certain nights to meet their "FENCES", outwardly respectable men who bought stolen goods cheaply and sold them on expensively, becoming richer than the thieves themselves. They lived a safer life too: for in those days many criminals ended their days on the GALLOWS, as horse stealing, highway robbery and many other offences carried the death penalty.

Benjamin Clarke was a little sneak thief who sometimes came to these meetings. He was not brave enough to arm himself with a pistol and rob the mail coaches, but would slip into churches and steal the odd candlestick, or seeing a housewife hanging out her washing in the back garden, would slip in through the front door and quickly snatch away any little valuable thing he could find. He rarely had anything which would interest the fences because he avoided taking anything which could lead him to the gallows, but on those rare occasions when he did have something of value, he would swagger and boast to the other thieves present of his success, jingling the silver coins he had been paid. Few people took much notice of Benjamin Clark however, and for this reason: thieves in those days were proud of their daring exploits, the riskier the undertaking, the greater the glory. Even the general public respected the brave highwaymen, thinking it was a sort of honour to be robbed by the more notorious of them.

So Benjamin Clarke found that when the highwaymen, cut-throats and their fences sat at the top table drinking toasts to one another, he was left at the other end of the room with the pick-pockets and shoplifters.

On a cold winter's night at one such meeting Benjamin had nothing to sell. He was sitting staring disconsolately into the fire, nursing a small pot of beer, when a well dressed man came and stood beside him. From his good clothes, and well fed looks, Benjamin supposed him to be a Fence. After a minute or so the well dressed man looked down at Benjamin and noting that he had nothing to sell, told him he needed to change his ways. That if he were to obtain a "Hand of Glory", his fortunes would improve. Benjamin looked puzzled, telling the man that he had never heard of a "HAND OF GLORY". The fence looked surprised at what he called "his ignorance" and leaning close to him, whispered that he should visit Betty Struthers of

Castleton at once and get her to make him one. Then the rich man turned away and walked out of the door.

Benjamin was intrigued by what the man had said, so the next day he made his way over the moors to Castleton. He asked where Betty Struthers lived, and was directed to a neat looking cottage by the village green. He went up to the door and was about to knock when it flew open, revealing Betty Struthers.

"So you've come about the Hand, eh? Come in".

Benjamin followed the woman into her cottage, and sat Down on the chair which she pointed out to him.

"IT'LL COST YOU TWENTY POUNDS", she said, "but it'll be worth it".

Now twenty pounds was as much as Benjamin earned in a year, and Betty, seeing the concern on his face, said: "It's all right; you look a trustworthy sort. You can pay me later".

Soon a deal was struck and Benjamin, after making a solemn promise to pay the money which he owed in twelve months time, left with his Hand of Glory.

The Hand of Glory
A Recipe for Thieves

Take the severed right hand of a hanged man, and remove all tendons and fat. Dry the hand in a mixture of salt, pepper and Saltpetre, then smoke it in a chimney for at least three weeks. In the meantime, form the fat from the hand into small candle.

When the hand is prepared, take to the house of a rich person, and place the hand on the doorstep with the candle in the palm of the hand, light it, and repeat the following lines:

> Let those who rest more deeply sleep
> Let those awake their vigils keep
> Oh hand of glory shed thy light
> Direct us to our spoil tonight

The people in the house will immediately fall into a deep slumber, the locks will open, and the house breaker may carry out his crime with no danger of detection.

Betty Struthers was an expert at making Hands of Glory, and they worked very well, so that Benjamin soon became a successful burglar, earning many times more than the twenty pounds he owed. Within two months he was sitting at the top table at the ale house, amongst the boldest of thieves, laughing
and drinking, admired by all.

But Benjamin was a GREEDY MAN, and as the time to pay Betty Struthers neared, he began to fret at the thought of paying her so much for what was "just a bit of cooking". Then an idea came to him. He realised that Betty could not complain to a magistrate if he refused to pay her, for although the laws against witchcraft had been done away with, claiming to be a witch was still punishable by a years imprisonment, and four sessions in "the stocks", where she would be pelted with rotten fruit. He also realised that although Betty was a powerful witch, and could use these powers against him, if he consulted a "WISEMAN", skilled in countering the spells of witches, he could obtain sufficient charms to make her incapable of harming him. So he paid a visit to a knowledgeable Wiseman in Scarborough, and was soon fully protected from the power of all witches at a fraction of the price he should have paid Betty.

So it was that at the end of the year, Betty Struthers waited vainly in her little cottage for Benjamin to appear.

The next morning she set out walking to Thirsk, and found Benjamin in the ale house. Betty glared at him, "Where's my money?" she said.

Benjamin clenched his thumb in his fist and shook it in her face.

"You'll get no money from me," he jeered, "look here!" and opening his coat he revealed the charms he had gathered to protect himself.

Betty turned and walked to the door and pausing there shouted "No good will come of it, MARK MY WORDS" and she left.

Benjamin was correct in believing that Betty Struthers could not harm him, but she was not entirely helpless. She dug up a little tin from her back garden, from which she took the tendons which she had removed from Benjamin's "Hand of Glory" during it's preparation. She rolled them in the leaf of a certain herb, and threw them, herb and tendon, into the fire.

That very night at midnight, shortly after Benjamin had climbed in through the window of yet another rich farmer's house, the fingers of the hand began to curl, snuffing out the candle in the palm: destroying the power of the hand forever. Just as he was peering into a draw, Benjamin felt something cold on the side of his head. It was the barrel of the outraged farmer's gun. A constable was called, and poor Benjamin was carried off to gaol.

At the next assizes, Benjamin appeared in court, and the "Hand of Glory" was produced as evidence against him, convincing the jury that he was an hardened, PROFESSIONAL CRIMINAL.

Found guilty, the judge felt that the whole weight of the law must be applied. Putting a black cloth over his wig, he looked gravely over at Benjamin and said:

"You are convicted of house-breaking, a felony of the first order. The sentence of this court is that you be taken from this place and to a place of execution, and there that you be hanged by the neck until you are dead, and may Christ have mercy on your soul."

And so we see him, as at the start of this tale, locked in the CONDEMNED CELL, sobbing in terror as Betty Struthers bargains with the hangman, keen to obtain the raw material for her next Hand of Glory.

JEANNIE *THE* HAG OF MULGRAVE WOODS

YOU might think that a young and eligible bachelor would shun the company of an old hag of a witch, but they do have there uses: the rent man comes for his money, but hops away penniless as a toad: you are hungry, the Devil pops down the chimney with a DELICIOUS ROAST CHICKEN. In short, a witch could provide a husband with the many physical comforts which we nowadays take for granted, but which in times past were hardly to be obtained by the very richest of folk.

ANDREW rode his old mare down towards MULGRAVE WOODS with these very comforts in mind. For in the woods, in a cave, lived Jeannie, the Hag of Mulgrave. He rubbed his hands with glee, drooling over the sumptuous meals he imagined he would soon be sharing with her: the tasty broths and steaming puddings; the vast sides of beef. And after the meal, perhaps, he could admire the TREASURES which he had heard she had gathered and heaped up in her cave. While as for her being his wife, why the cave was dark and shadowy enough to hide the full extent of her ugliness, and if she chewed on herbs, it would mask the legendary foul reek of her breath, should she decide to kiss him tenderly.

Andrew gave no thought to her equally legendary FOUL TEMPER, or the fact that her treasures were supposed to come from the travellers she had ROBBED AND EATEN. For was not Andrew a young and handsome chap? A fellow who cut a fine figure on his horse? A man who could easily be mistaken for a knight or nobleman?

Andrew's horse entered the woods, crossing the little stream which was in ancient times dedicated to a vengeful pagan goddess (some said that Jeannie was that goddess). The woods were dark, and the thick layer of dead leaves underfoot deadened the sound of the horse's hooves. No birds were singing. Andrew looked around him. He was a little nervous now. He tried to shout "Jeannie!" but only a hoarse whisper came from his mouth. Feeling a little foolish at his fear, he cleared his throat and shouted at the top of his voice:

"JEANNIE, COME HERE YOU OLD HAG!
LET ME KISS YOUR LIPS".

For a second there was silence, then a rustling in the undergrowth. Andrew smiled, waiting for his "sweetheart" to appear. His "sweetheart" *did* appear. Wild-eyed. Sharp-toothed. Furious. Jeannie leaped from behind a bush with a wild cry, slashing the branches with her sharp claws. Andrew had been preparing some gallant remark or other with which to win her heart, but on seeing her, terrified by the sight, he whipped his horse furiously to get away. She pursued him, snarling, gaining each second.

Andrew had heard it said that witches could not cross RUNNING-WATER, so in desperation drove his horse straight at the little stream, Spurring the animal on, he made made a giant leap for the water just as Jeannie caught him up. Her claws slashed at the horse, cutting it clean in two. Andrew and the front part of his horse landed on the other side of the stream. The front end of the old mare, so terrified of the hag, continued to gallop on it's remaining two legs until it reached the safety of Whitby.

Meanwhile Jeannie tossed the back end of the horse over her shoulder and lapping up the fresh blood as she went, took it home to cook for supper.

To this day it is said that Jeannie lives in the woods, and will come out if you shout her name. You would be well advised to stand very close to the bridge before you do, however, even in this SCEPTICAL age, when some of us no longer believe in witches.

OLD MULGRAVE CASTLE

NANNY GARBUTT
OF GREAT AYTON

IN days past it was common for people to approach witches to cast spells on their enemies, and it was on this errand that a scruffy fellow named JOHNNY SIMPSON went to visit an old witch named NANNY GARBUTT who lived in Great Ayton.

Johnny Simpson was a lazy fellow: he was employed on a local farm, but would never do a full day's work. The farmer would send him to collect the sheep, and find him asleep under a tree, or set him to chopping turnips then discover him sitting with the pretty young dairymaid, tickling her chin or drinking milk. The farmer had threatened him with sacking several times, and he was now on a "last warning". As a result Mary, his girlfriend, thinking that he could never look after her, had left him and was to marry a hardworking young man called Tom Smith. Johnny was very upset, but too lazy to try and win back his sweetheart. He decided, instead, to spoil their wedding by obtaining a curse from Nanny Garbutt.

Nanny Garbutt, smiled happily at Johnny Simpson as he told her he wanted to spoil a wedding, for, she said, nothing would make her happier than to blight the life of a young couple! Hunching over the fire, eyes GLEAMING EVILLY, she suggested striking the bride blind on her wedding day, or perhaps giving the groom a hare lip as he uttered his vows.

Johnny looked nervously at the hag: he had not thought of anything nearly so bad. Instead, he suggested, the groom should drop the wedding ring in the graveyard, the wedding cake could have to much salt in it, or maybe they might argue on the way out of church.

Old Nanny Garbutt slowly turned her head towards Johnny, a look of utter disgust and disappointment on her face. She would have no part in making such feeble spells, she said, grinding the blackened stumps of her teeth furiously. Handing him her broom, she told him that she would give him a "do it yourself" charm to bring about minor mishaps at the wedding. His instructions were simple: he must go to Ayton Bridge at midnight, wave Nanny's broom over his head 3 times, walk backwards into the grave yard there, gather some soil, then wash his hands in the old well and leave Nanny's broom neatly by the side of it.

At midnight, Johnny went as instructed to Ayton Bridge, yawning and dragging his feet. He began to carry out the ceremony. Having waved the broom and gathered the soil, he was too lazy and scruffy to wash his hands, and so went home, carelessly throwing the broom into a nearby stream.

Now witches take a particular pride in their brooms, and when Johnny threw hers away, Nanny immediately knew, waking up with a shock. She poured some water into a brass bowl while uttering a charm and, looking in, saw reflected, her broom in the stream, and Johnny, dirty hands and all, walking home. Nanny's eyes glinted red with rage. Muttering a strange curse, she threw a handful of salt into her smoldering fire. Then she looked back into her bowl and saw with satisfaction, Johnny, surrounded by hundreds of evil demons, and the broom, flying swiftly through the air, WHACKING him with painful blows to his head. The demons closed in and were about to grab him, when the broom flew between his legs and rose up high over their heads. Johnny clung desperately to the broom as it flew over the hills, the furious demons in hot pursuit. The broom swooped through woods, the branches whipping poor Johnny until his blood ran in streams, and his clothes were ripped to rags. It plunged into the sea, freezing him. It bounced into clumps of nettles, covering him in stings. But still he clung desperately to the broom, for close behind were the demons, razor sharp claws outstretched towards him.

Suddenly, towards dawn, the broom dropped from the sky and lay still on the ground. Johnny falling heavily, lay for a second, his arms and body aching. Then he saw the demons, closing in on him. He leapt to his feet, and sprang away as fast as he could. After running for ten miles he came to Roseberry topping, a great hill near Guisborough. Exhausted as he was, Johnny ran up the steep side of the hill, trying to keep ahead of the demons. At the top, he saw the sun rise, and looking back over his shoulder, saw the demons fade away and disappear.

After this long night of torment, all of Johnny's jobs on the farm seemed, in comparison, easy, and he became an excellent worker.

Mary's wedding passed off without incident, and was followed a few weeks later by Johnny's, who walked down the isle with the pretty milk maid from his farm.

ANN ALLAN
AND HER STOOL

IN the 1780s, Ann Allan moved to Ugthorpe, a little village between Whitby and Staithes. At that time it was the custom for farmers to run a "pig club" between them: each would keep a pig, and would take turns in killing it and sharing out the meat.

Ann Allan surprised every one by announcing that she wanted to join the club, for she lived in a little cottage with a tiny garden which everyone thought was too small to keep a pig. People were even more surprised when her pig proved to be the BIGGEST, JUICIEST BEAST to have been slaughtered in the history of the pig club.

The mystery as to how Ann Allan succeeded in growing such a fine animal was the main subject of conversation in the village for weeks afterwards, but if anyone asked her for her secret she simply tapped her nose and winked, her mouth firmly closed.

Now in those days, winter was a hard time for food ran short, both man and beast becoming lean and thin. Imagine the amazement of the villagers then, when six months later, and in the middle of the winter, Ann's next pig came to be slaughtered, and it was yet larger and fatter than the one before. Again, Ann kept quiet about how she fattened her pigs, and the mystery of how she did so would have remained a mystery forever, had it not been for Tom Smith. Tom was one of her neighbours, and joked with his wife that Ann Allan might be a witch and be using witchcraft to fatten her pig.

Well, Ann got to hear of Tom's jest, and was very angry. And this is strange, for Ann *WAS* indeed a witch, and *was* using witchcraft to fatten her pig. She had a little STOOL, and had only to say the name of one of her neighbour's cows for some of its milk to flow out of the leg of the stool. This milk she fed to her pig, fattening it up nicely. Until that time she had been taking a little milk from each of her neighbours in turn, but now, to revenge herself, decided to steal only from Tom's cow, SORREL.

Within a few days Sorrel's milk had begun to dry up, and this was soon the talk of the village. Ann Allan visited Tom's house several times, outwardly to express her sympathy, but inwardly to gloat. So sympathetic was she, that Tom became suspicious of her, and began to think again about his joke about Ann being a witch, and to wonder if there might be some foundation to it.

Tom had heard that witches have a "FAMILIAR.", a little demon in the form of an animal which does the witch's bidding, He decided to keep watch over Sorrel, thinking that maybe he might catch the familiar, in the form of a hedgehog perhaps, sneaking along to milk her under the cover of darkness. For one long, cold, night Tom sat up in his field, but with no luck and, to make matters worse, as he got up from his hiding place, stretching, shivering and yawning, he noticed Ann Allan looking out of her window at him,

"Thou'll see nowt there!" she sneered

Tom led Sorrel down to the yard, and tried to milk her, but with no luck. The smug look on Ann's face came back to him then, and in a temper he went to her door, banging on it, shouting for Ann to open up. Other neighbours began to gather, one or two telling Tom to go home, thinking he was drunk. This so enraged him that he kicked open the door and stormed in where he found Ann was sitting by the fire, looking very innocent indeed.

"Save me from this madman!" she cried.

Tom snatched up a little stool which was standing in the corner. He shook it menacingly at her and shouted:

"YOU'VE BEEN STEALING MILK FROM SORREL!"

He would have said more but just then a stream of milk jetted from one of the legs of the stool onto the floor. ANN ALLAN WAS UNDONE!

Soon the whole village was assembled to look at the amazing stool. As each farmer called out the name of his favourite cow he found that a stream of milk appeared from the leg of the stool. Nobody there doubted that she was truly a witch.

Perhaps because Ugthorpe is near to Staithes, the villagers took a gentle line with Ann. They built a great fire just outside the village, and she was made to throw her charmed stool into it. Then for three Sundays she had to visit the church in her underwear, and confess her crimes in public, promising never to repeat them.

This was apparently the end of the matter as far as the villagers were concerned, for several years later, in 1779, the parish registers show that Ann married a local man called Robert Atkinson, and lived happily in the parish for many years.

Nanny Appleby
of Ripon

IN a little decaying cottage, just outside Ripon, lived Nanny Appleby, a woman regarded locally as a witch.

She certainly looked the part, for she was the ugliest old crone you could imagine. Her nose and chin were so big and curved that they would bump each other when she chewed a crust of bread. Great HAIRY WARTS as big as gooseberries dotted her face, and when she smiled, which was surprisingly often, it revealed her teeth. These were small, pointed, and yellow, but her gums were big and red. Her most striking feature, however, were her eyes, they were great big bulging things, and you would think that if anyone patted her on the back, they must surely fall out. Her eyes were also crossed, and this bulging and crossing made it seem as if they were trying to peep at each other over her huge nose.

Nanny had lived in her little cottage for so long that no one could even remember where she had come from, though some people thought she was from HARROGATE, (where, they said, everyone looks like her). Strange to say Nanny was quite content with her face, for mirrors in those days were rare and expensive objects, which meant she rarely had to see herself, and it was everyone else who had to suffer.

As it happens, Nanny Appleby was a witch, but not a bad one. She generally used her powers to make herbal medicines and cures, which she sold in the market place in Ripon. Often times when she was in the market, a local lad called TOM MOSS would abuse Nanny Parson, calling her horrible names, thrusting his fist, under her face, with the thumb clenched in the palm of his hand - a sign implying that she was a witch, but could not harm him. Nanny, however, kept her peace.

One day, Nanny was called out to an emergency, a poor widow's son being dangerously ill. She packed up her bag of herbal remedies and set off for the widow's house

Tom Moss, seeing her in such a hurry, followed her down the street, imitating her limp and shouting crude oaths after her. When she entered the widow's house, Tom pressed up against the window, blowing his cheeks up, and pulling ugly faces.

Inside the cottage the widow's son was in a very serious condition, cold but sweating, more dead than alive.

Now tradition has it that occasionally a DEMON escapes from Hell, and comes onto the earth to cause trouble. It is the job of passing angels to turn such demons to stone. As a result the demons, fearful of the angels, usually take refuge in the BELLIES of unfortunate humans, tormenting them, and this was the case with the widow's son. When Nanny Appleby looked down the boy's throat, she could see the demon looking out, grinning at her. The demon's grin disappeared very quickly when he saw her pour some holy water down the boy's throat. It jumped out of the child's mouth at great speed and flew around the room. Nanny Appleby grabbed his ankle and pulled him out through the door. Either the demon was stronger than she expected, or Nanny had a plan to be revenged on the boy who had tormented her for so long, for she let go, and the demon, looking round desperately for refuge, saw Tom Moss, his mouth invitingly open with amazement and in a flash, it disappeared down into the boy's belly. A belly which he found so very much to his taste, that he decided to stay there, permanently.

Tom was not very pleased with his new lodger, for it teased and tormented him as much as he had teased and tormented Nanny Appleby, driving him first to the madhouse, and then to the river Ure, where he drowned himself in despair.

BLACK MEG
OF INGLEBY

INGLEBY GREENHOW is a pretty village in Bilsdale, and was once the home to a particularly evil witch known as Black Meg.

Unlike most witches, for much of her life Black Meg did not have a cat, said she did not like them, said they got hairs everywhere. Besides, she had a pet serpent or "Worm" as they were known, a great black monster, half snake half dragon, which lived in a cave under her house and acted as a form of central heating by breathing fire.

Then one year she became a witch who liked cats - BLACK CATS. Lots of them. Black Meg took a liking for black cats for a very good reason: she had discovered that they could be sold to the wives of fishermen in Scarborough, for the women there believed that black cats had a powerful magic in them which could keep their husbands safe at sea.

That year no black cat was safe within miles of Black Meg, for she took to scouring the countryside and stealing any she could find. To conceal her crimes, she painted the cats white hoping that no one would suspect that she had taken their pet.

When it was time for the fair, she threw all the cats into a large sack, and threw the sack into a stream to wash off the white paint, then she carried the lot dripping, hissing, scratching and fighting to Scarborough, where she sold them for immense profit.

The second year, Meg decided to increase her profits by stealing cats of all different colours, and painting them black. Unfortunately a shower fell at the fair, washing the cats clean and revealing her ploy. Black Meg was lucky to survive, for she was beaten black and blue and nearly lynched by the enraged population.

The third year, there were no cats for Meg to steal, so she came up with quite a different plan. She employed a couple of other witches to help her with a very special and powerful cat-creating spell. The spell needed all three witches to assemble high up on the moors, besides an ancient pillar or Monolith, and there summon up all sorts of dreadful elves, snakes and ravens.

Unfortunately this spell needed one very special ingredient: a human baby. At the height of the cat-creating ceremony, the child would be picked up by its ankle, swung vigorously round the witch's head, and thrown into the fire, to emerge from the flames seconds later as a slightly singed black cat.

Soon the babies of Ingleby began to disappear, as Meg assembled herself a fine collection of black cats, which she kept locked up in a dark cupboard under the stairs of her little cottage. The villagers called in a "Wiseman" from Scarborough to solve the mystery of the missing babies. He followed Meg one dark night and saw for himself the dreadful cat-making ceremony.

Now the solution to the problem of the missing babies was simple according to the Wiseman - at least in theory. The cats must be taken from Black Meg, and put into the church, where the spell would be broken. However, the practical problems were great: the Wiseman knew all about the Worm which lived in Meg's cellar, and feared that she would take her revenge on the villagers, by unleashing it upon them. They needed, he said, some brave knight or hero to fight the Worm.

Well the village idiot, a man by the name of CHRISTOPHER FURZE, was listening to the Wiseman, and he did not understand what the locals meant by a "Worm". Thinking they needed someone to fight a little earthworm, he pulled out a pocket knife and offered his services. Everyone was surprised by his great courage, and decided to go to Meg's house immediately before he could change his mind. As quietly as they could, the villagers sneaked in and removed the cats from their little cupboard. Meg, who had been having a snooze, woke when the door slammed behind the last of them, and finding her cats gone, let out her dreadful Worm to be revenged.

The great creature squeezed its massive coils out of the front door, and saw Christopher, armed with his little knife, his face turning white, his knees beginning to shake. Old Meg rubbed her hands with glee as she saw the creature slither up the street toward the quaking fool, smoke and flames bellowing from its nostrils. The village idiot was too scared to move, and the creature was soon upon him. It opened its mouth and was about to bite him in two when Black Meg called "That's it, get him!" The worm, hearing its master's voice was distracted and glanced round, giving Christopher one chance, which, fool though he was, he took, of thrusting his little knife into the eye of the Worm. Immediately the creature began to writhe about, mortally wounded. while a great sound of babies crying rose in the church, as the cats turned back to babies.

Some people say that Meg's house burst into flames, and that Meg herself was seen being dragged off to Hell by the Devil. Whether this is true or not is hard to say, but it is true to say that you will not find Meg or her house, nor any "Worms" in Ingleby Greenhowe today.

THE END

'WHERE ARE THEY? GONE?'
                    MACBETH

Also by
The Cædmon Storytellers

13 GHOST STORIES FROM WHITBY Based on the folklore of this quaint seaside town, it was the Cædmon Storytellers first book and is still turning hairs grey! More ghosts and ghouls than you can shake a stick at. But beware, some of these ghosts don't take very well to people shaking sticks at them!

THE HAUNTED COAST Following the Phenomenal success of 13 Ghost Stories from Whitby, the Cædmon Storytellers continued their research along the whole length of the Yorkshire coast, leaving no dank and eerie crypt unexplored, visiting (and drinking in) every haunted pub they could find to bring you The Haunted Coast, thirteen of the best Traditional Ghost Stories from the Humber to the Tees.

13 TRADITIONAL GHOST STORIES FROM LINCOLNSHIRE The Cædmon Storytellers took a holiday from Yorkshire and visited 'The County of Fear' - Lincolnshire - possibly the most haunted county in England.

THE GHOSTS AND GHOULS OF THE EAST RIDING How do they do it? *Why do they do it?* The Caedmon Storytellers have braved the sound of screaming skulls in haunted houses, dodged wicked witches in their flea-infested hovels and waited for the midnight hour in many a wayside inn where, amazingly, pint after pint of foaming beer disappeared before their very eyes!

The caedmon Storytellers, still drenched in sweat and shaking, bring you **13 TRADITIONAL GHOST STORIES FROM NORFOLK** - a county dripping with gore and ghosts.

Eyes wide with terror, the Caedmon Storytellers have survived, but only just, to bring you **THE GHOSTS AND GHOULS OF YORK**, the world's most haunted city. Read it if you dare...

THOU SHALT NOT SUFFER A WITCH TO LIVE

Exodus 22:18

IF ALL OF US HAVE NOT CONFESSED *TO BE*
WITCHES, THAT IS ONLY BECAUSE WE HAVE
NOT ALL BEEN TORTURED

Freidrich Spee, Jesuit priest

Printed in Great Britain
by Amazon

82684745R00038